SITTI'S SECRETS

by Naomi Shihab Nye • illustrated by Nancy Carpenter

Aladdin Paperbacks

First Aladdin Paperbacks edition October 1997
Text copyright © 1994 by Naomi Shihab Nye
Illustrations copyright © 1994 by Nancy Carpenter

Aladdin Paperbacks
An imprint of Simon & Schuster Children's Publishing Division
1230 Avenue of the Americas, New York, NY 10020

Also available in a Simon & Schuster Books for Young Readers edition.
Designed by Christy Hale
The text of this book was set in collage bold.
The illustrations were rendered in mixed media.
Printed and bound in China 0314 LEE

30 29 28 27 26 25 24 23 22 21

The Library of Congress has cataloged the hardcover edition as follows:
Nye, Naomi Shihab.
Sitti's Secrets / by Naomi Shihab Nye ; illustrated by Nancy Carpenter. — 1st ed.
p.   cm.
Summary: A young girl describes a visit to see her grandmother in a Palestinian
village on the West Bank.
ISBN 978-0-02-768460-5
[1. Grandmothers—Fiction.   2. Palestinian Arabs—Israel—Fiction.]
I. Carpenter, Nancy, ill.   II. Title.
PZ7.N976Si   1994
[E]—dc20   93-19742

ISBN 978-0-689-81706-9 (Aladdin pbk.)

For Sitti Khadra Shihab Idais Al-Zer of Palestine,
still alive at 105,
and all grandmothers everywhere who give our lives
gravity and light

—N.S.N.

To Victoria, David, and Chico,
and in memory of Nahiza Badran Karaman

—N.C.

My Grandmother lives on the other side of the earth. When I have daylight, she has night. When our sky grows dark, the sun is peeking through her window and brushing the bright lemons on her lemon tree. I think about this when I am going to sleep.

"Your turn!" I say.

Between us are many miles
of land and water.
Between us are fish and cities
and buses and fields

and presidents and clotheslines
and trucks and stop signs and
signs that say DO NOT ENTER
and grocery stores and benches
and families and deserts and
a million trees.

Once I went to visit my grandmother. My grandmother and I do not speak the same language. We talked through my father, as if he were a telephone, because he spoke both our languages and could translate what we said.

I called her *Sitti,* which means Grandma in Arabic. She called me *habibi,* which means darling. Her voice danced as high as the whistles of birds. Her voice giggled and whooshed like wind going around corners. She had a thousand rivers in her voice.

A few curls of dark hair peeked out of her scarf on one side, and a white curl peeked out on the other side. I wanted her to take off the scarf so I could see if her hair was striped.

Soon we had invented our own language together. Sitti pointed at my stomach to ask if I was hungry. I pointed to the door to ask if she wanted to go outside. We walked to the fields to watch men picking lentils. We admired the sky with hums and claps.

We crossed the road to buy milk from a family that kept one spotted cow. I called the cow *habibi,* and it winked at me. We thanked the cow, with whistles and clicks, for the fresh milk that we carried home in Sitti's little teapot.

Every day I played with my cousins, Fowzi, Sami, Hani, and Hendia from next door. We played marbles together in their courtyard. Their marbles were blue and green and spun through the dust like planets. We didn't need words to play marbles.

My grandmother lives on the other side
of the earth. She eats cucumbers for
breakfast, with yogurt and bread.
She bakes the big, flat bread
in a round, old oven next
to her house. A fire burns
in the middle.

She pats the dough between her hands
and presses it out to bake on a flat
black rock in the center of the oven.
My father says she has been
baking that bread for
a hundred years.

My grandmother and I sat under her lemon tree in the afternoons, drinking lemonade with mint in it. She liked me to pick bunches of mint for her. She liked to press her nose into the mint and sniff.

Some days we stuffed little zucchini squash with rice for dinner. We sang *habibi, habibi* as we stacked them in a pan. We cracked almonds and ate apricots, called *mish-mish*, while we worked.

One day Sitti took off her scarf and shook out her hair.
She washed her hair in a tub right there under the sun. Her
hair surprised me by being very long. And it *was* striped!
She said it got that way all by itself. I helped her brush it
out while it dried. She braided it and pinned the braid up
before putting on the scarf again.

I felt as if I knew a secret.

In the evenings we climbed the stairs to the roof of Sitti's house to look at the sky, smell the air, and take down the laundry. My grandmother likes to unpin the laundry in the evening so she can watch the women of the village walking back from the spring with jugs of water on their heads. She used to do that, too. My father says the women don't really need to get water from the spring anymore, but they like to. It is something from the old days they don't want to forget.

On the day my father and I had to leave, everyone cried and cried. Even my father kept blowing his nose and walking outside. I cried hard when Sitti held my head against her shoulder. My cousins gave me a sack of almonds to eat on the plane. Sitti gave me a small purse she had made. She had stitched a picture of her lemon tree onto the purse with shiny thread. She popped the almonds into my purse and pulled the drawstrings tight.

Our plane flew to the other side of the world.
I remember the tattoos on my grandmother's hands.
They look like birds flying away. My father says she has
had those tattoos for a hundred years.
I think about Sitti's old green trunk in the corner of her
room. It has a padlock on it—she wears the key on a green

ribbon around her neck. She keeps my grandfather's rings in there, and her gold thread, and needles, and pieces of folded-up blue velvet from old dresses, and two small leather books, and a picture of my father before he came to the United States, and a picture of my parents on their wedding day, and a picture of me when I was a baby, smiling and very fat. Did I really look like that?

When I got home, I wrote a letter to the president of the United States.

Dear Mr. President,

My grandmother on the other side of the world has a lemon tree that whispers secrets. She talks to it and gives it water from her own drinking glass. She guesses the branch where lemons will grow next. All the old men and women of her village take good care of their trees. Some have fig trees with shiny leaves. Some have almond trees covered with white blossoms that fall down on the road like snow.

Last night when I watched the news on TV, I felt worried. If the people of the United States could meet Sitti, they'd like her, for sure. You'd like her, too.

My grandmother can read the stars and the moon and the clouds. She can read dreams and tea leaves in the bottom of a cup. She even said she could read good luck on my forehead.

Mr. President, I wish you my good luck in your very hard job. I vote for peace. My grandmother votes with me.

Sincerely,
Mona

Does my grandmother know what will happen in
the world?
Does the world have a forehead?

Sometimes I think the world is a huge body tumbling in space, all curled up like a child sleeping. People are far apart, but connected.

My grandmother lives on the other side of the earth.
While I am dreaming, she rises from her fluffy bed and
steps out her door to check the lemons growing on her tree.
The first thing she does every day is say good morning
to her lemons.

All day the leafy shadow of her tree will grow and
change on her courtyard wall. She will move with its shade.
When she sleeps, she will dream of me.